FALLING INTO PLACE

THE LUMINATED THREADS
A PREQUEL NOVELLA

BOOKS BY LAUREL WANROW

THE WINDBORNE SERIES ~ FOR YOUNG ADULTS

Double Rescue (prequel novella)

The Witch of the Meadows

Guardian of the Pines

Lost Whisperer of the Seas

Keepers of the Sea Cliffs

Solstice Gifts (holiday short story)

THE LUMINATED THREADS SERIES ~ FOR AGES 15 & UP

The Unraveling, Volume One

The Twisting, Volume Two

The Binding, Volume Three

The Luminated Threads Volumes 1-3 Box Set

Falling into Place (prequel novella)

SCIENCE FICTION ROMANCE ~ FOR ADULTS

Passages

For the most current release list, see the 'Books' link on Laurel's website, www.laurelwanrow.com.

FALLING INTO PLACE

THE LUMINATED THREADS
A PREQUEL NOVELLA

LAUREL WANROW

Sprouting Star Press

Copy Edit by Joyce Lamb
Cover Design by Deranged Doctor Design
Created with Vellum

Wanrow, Laurel

Falling into Place / Laurel Wanrow. ~ 1st ed.
ISBN 978-1-943469-30-7

First Edition: March 2023

For my fellow cottagecore readers who want more farm life!

CHAPTER 1

Spring 1867
Peaks District, England

A hand reached into the mixing bowl as Mary Clare Pemberton folded in the dried apples. In a practiced move, she blocked her youngest sister with her elbow.

"Why can't I taste it?" howled Mary Grace.

"Do you see that recipe? Where does it say, 'Mix in germs liberally'? Go away."

With a flounce, Mary Grace ran from their family's farm kitchen, probably for the weaving room. But Ma wouldn't object to her disciplining the six-year-old.

Mary Clare began spooning batter into the buttered tin cups. Her sister Mary Ellen arrived to refill Ma's tea, complained the kettle wasn't hot, then accidentally turned off the gas. Mary Clare relit the tricky burner, but the almost-teenager stomped out instead of waiting. Mary Clare sighed.

She'd finished dropping dollops when Granny hobbled in. "Did I tell you raspberry? It's the birthday girl's favorite."

Mary Clare had discussed the order with Granny's friend. "I

reminded Mrs. Silvie no one has raspberries this early in the spring. She agreed cinnamon apple was fine." Mary Clare scraped the bowl while Granny harrumphed, checked the kettle and settled at the table to wait.

"In the old days, we'd have plenty of dried on hand," Granny said. "Right up to the next season."

"You had only three children, Granny. Seven means—"

Returning, Mary Ellen chimed in with Mary Clare on the oft-repeated family mantra, "You make do."

While Mary Ellen refilled Ma's mug and Granny's—thank the Creator—Mary Clare spooned cinnamon and sugar over the muffin batter. Only five of the girls still lived at home on their parents' sheep farm, but that meant the summer fruits Ma and Granny put up lasted merely a month longer. The vegetables, of course, lasted forever. Mary Clare should be out of the house already, like her two oldest sisters, but patching together part-time cook's assistant jobs in Chapel Hollow didn't cover living expenses. And…her Knack was an issue.

If only she had a Knack for growing plants, the most in-demand skill in the rural Farmlands shire. Her Knack wasn't the kind one mentioned in conversation, polite or otherwise. Folks outside the family assumed she wasn't a Knack-bearer. The magical Knacks weren't everything. Without one, her oldest sister, Mary Alice, had secured a job at Wellspring Collective, a cooperative farm at the edge of town, managing their canning inventory and shipping. She and their second-oldest sister, Mary Beth, who had a grower Knack, shared a room in Wellspring's bunkhouse.

As Mary Clare slid the tins into the oven, Mary Grace darted in and swiped the batter spoon.

"Soon I'll have a job with no little sisters underfoot!" called Mary Clare, with a glance at the clock. She hardly needed to. Daily baking had ingrained an automatic thirty-minute reminder into her head.

During the baking, she washed up to be ready to deliver the muffins while they were still warm, so a customer wouldn't hesitate to hand over the payment. Now if only she had that spoon to finish up—

The back door burst open, and Mary Alice rushed in. "You're here!" she said breathlessly as she grasped Mary Clare's shoulders, her eyes gleaming. "I volunteered to fetch you as soon as I heard. Come on!"

"Heard what?" Granny asked before Mary Clare could. "Not trouble?"

No, it wasn't trouble. Mary Clare could sense that through her Knack. Excitement and joy rolled off of Mary Alice, and Mary Clare forgot her lecture about kitchen cleanliness and reached up on tippy-toes to hug her taller sister. Mary Clare bounced twice on the spot. "You're thrilled for me? Why?"

Mary Alice lifted a finger, and trepidation flowed forth. "Ah-ah. You can't! Not now."

Mary Clare's Knack shifted again to match her sister's emotion. "Darn it all, I had *no* warning." Frowning, she backed away, batting the air between them as Mary Alice moved her hands in the boxing motion Ma always made to indicate Mary Clare should ward her Knack.

She pressed her forehead, bringing up barriers to block incoming feelings. "I don't need reminders," she huffed. "I secure it when I'm anywhere else." Because if she didn't, and swayed the wrong stranger's emotions, she'd be labeled a Basin witch and banned from the magical Blighted Basin valley forever.

Thus, she'd lived at home longer than most young women, perfecting her warding. But seeing her sisters' freedom swelled her urge for independence and spurred her goal of living outside their tight-knit family.

The risk would be worth it. "Ugh. I'm so *tired* of family interfering," she muttered.

Mary Alice sighed. "Consider it for your own good. Get changed and come."

"What exactly is the news?" asked Granny.

"Wellspring's kitchen assistant has up and left with no notice," squealed Mary Alice. "Rumor is, she either got a job at the new station diner up at Cross Corners, or she's run off with an animacambire, but our cook isn't saying. The best news is, Mrs. Betsy came to ask me if Mary Clare might be available."

"To replace her?" Mary Clare asked breathlessly. This was the answer to her dreams.

Mary Alice shook her head. "That wasn't mentioned. She needs kitchen help *now*. With the new growers who came on, and planting season in full swing, Mrs. Betsy is beside herself. You're every bit as proficient as that girl was, and I think you and Mrs. Betsy would suit, if only you keep…"

Mary Clare didn't wait for the rest. She spun for the stairs. In her room, she changed into her newest bib and brace and a clean flannel shirt. As for what to do with her braided hair, she hesitated. Curly hair never behaved. With no time for more, she found a pressed kerchief, brushed back the wayward red strands from her face and covered the lot. Perfect. She pounded down the stairs, and the sweet scent of browning sugar met her.

"No," she cried. "The muffins for Mrs. Silvie!"

But Granny already had the tins out of the oven. Breathing her thanks, Mary Clare grabbed one tray and lifted each muffin onto the cooling rack.

"Is she expecting them now?" An edge of worry seeped into Mary Alice's question.

Oh, dear. "Yes." Mary Clare pressed a hand to her forehead and re-warded her Knack. This was all too exciting, and she'd best do that immediately. Forming a plan, she arranged the muffins in the flat basket she used for delivering baked goods, already lined with a fresh cloth. "Mary Ellen?" she called. "Would you deliver the muffins to Mrs. Silvie?"

Mary Ellen appeared in the doorway with a thoughtful expression, like she had no idea what the errand involved, when she'd tagged along numerous times. "For half your fee."

"One-tenth," snapped Mary Clare. "Otherwise, I deliver them myself and am late to Wellspring." She leveled a raised-brow-stare at the twelve-year-old.

"Now, Mary Ellen, be a dear and help your sister," cooed Mary Alice. "Think on it a minute. If she makes a good impression and is offered this position, Mary Delia will surely move into her empty room, leaving you a room to yourself."

Her sister's excited gasp as she ran to the coat closet said she hadn't thought that far ahead. Mary Clare rolled her eyes and followed to don her own woolen jacket.

The trio left the house and crossed under the cherry trees to the gate. She took a deep breath. The blossoms hadn't opened yet, but white buds capped the branches, and the promise of their sweet fragrance was in the air. Mary Alice held open the gate, and Mary Clare handed Mary Ellen the basket. "Thank you for your help."

Mary Ellen nodded. "One-tenth." With the basket held carefully in both hands, she set off, then called over her shoulder, "Go, get that job."

"I certainly plan to." She checked her Knack wards once more.

KNEELING on the concrete floor of Wellspring's workshop, Rivley Slipwing pecked a screwdriver at the dirt wedged between the gears of a machine's leg joint. How had a grower ruined a perfectly fine clockwork spider after only two days in the field? Gravel showered down, but didn't clear the mechanism. Rivley pressed his lips tight and got to his feet. At the workbench, he found an ice pick, started back, then fetched a canvas drop cloth.

He lifted the spider applicator onto the spread canvas and brought in another. Both new growers had complained the clockwork legs weren't agile enough to walk the planting rows on the sloped hillsides. They were.

Under his questioning, one fellow confessed his machine had rolled down the slope planted in spinach and into a gully. Rivley knew that field quite well, since until a month ago he'd been one of the raptor shifters patrolling the new plantings from the air and picking off mice and other farm vermin. In a year of flights, he'd never seen a machine *roll*.

The ice pick fit perfectly between the small sprockets, dislodging sprinkles of powder. He pulled over a crate and settled into the work, flicking out grit before dousing the joint with oil to flush the remaining dirt. He bent the joint to expose a different section of the gears and wiggled the pointed tool into those spaces.

The rear legs weren't as tightly compacted as the front two. He tried to imagine the fall. Forward, like onto its knees?

A *thump* interrupted his thoughts. Outside the shop, Master Brightwell had dropped his leather travel case into a waiting cart. The older dark-skinned man with springy white hair strode in with a smaller case.

Wellspring's head mechanic—and Rivley's mentor—shook his head at the debris under the machine. "Good morning, Mr. Slipwing. Any hope of returning that equipment to Mr. Hortens' workers this morning?"

"Well, no gears appear out of alignment."

"Several hours, then, a morning's annoyance. Don't let our spiders go out again until you've instructed the growers and watched them practice here in the farmyard."

"Didn't they have training with Mr. Hortens?"

Master Brightwell nodded as he unfolded wire-rimmed glasses and put them on. "Most assuredly, they did. However, that doesn't mean the new hires paid enough mind." He went to the workbench. "Taking a few of my own tools so I can inspect any potential purchase as I wish. Duplicates here of everything, so I won't leave you short." Master Brightwell sounded excited as he dropped the tools into his case.

Who wouldn't be? The farm sale might be a day's travel across Blighted Basin, but the poster listed all sorts of machines. Master Brightwell had his eye on a steam lift, a machine purported to lift a worker to a tree's upper branches to aid in picking fruit. If it worked well, they hoped to reproduce another before the cherries ripened a month from now.

Master Brightwell came to the opposite side of the spider machine, making a cursory check of its oil before he returned his glasses to their pocket and tucked the tool case under one arm. "I leave the workshop operations in your capable hands, Mr. Slipwing. I wouldn't feel as comfortable traveling without you here. Address the inventory as you can between Mr. Hortens' needs for the growers."

Rivley rose and wiped his hands on a rag he kept in his leather apron. "With any luck, this is the worst that will come through, sir. I plan to have those stalls sorted and organized before your return. I'll be anxious to inspect everything you find."

Master Brightwell smiled. "Perhaps next year, Wellspring will have resources to bring on a second apprentice, allowing us to attend sales together. You have a mind for mechanics, Mr. Slipwing, aided by your sharp eyesight and hearing."

"Thank you, sir. Have a good trip." Rivley extended his hand, and the inventor shook it.

A year ago, he never would have dreamed the inner workings of a machine could make sense to an animacambire raised to protect the safety of their hidden valley. Everything about the Farmlands was so different than his shapeshifter home in the rugged Black Mountains lining the southern edge of Blighted Basin. He'd never seen a mechanical device until he and his best friend, Daeryn Darkcoat, escaped the aftermath of a tragic accident down those rocky slopes. Finding the advertisement seeking 'cambire guards for Wellspring Collective had opened their eyes to a different life—one with a new and exciting future, in his case. If he learned enough during his apprenticeship with Master Brightwell, one day he could study at a mechanics' institute and run his own shop. First, he had an obligation to resolve with Daeryn.

CHAPTER 2

Mary Clare dashed into Wellspring's kitchen and grabbed another dish to ferry to the dining room.

"It's noon," Mrs. Betsy Campbell called, her short, white hair waving in time to her vigorous mashing of baked squash. "Please ring the bell, duck. Then this squash will be ready to serve."

Hustling, Mary Clare pivoted and headed for the kitchen's outer door. Her prior work at Wellspring had taught her it was far quicker to go outside to the bell than navigate the big farmhouse.

Unfamiliar workers were queued, and many smiled at her. When she reached the bell pole, she figured out why—she still held a giant wooden bowl of rolls. Grasping the rope with one hand, she managed a low *thunk*, not the usual loud peal.

Ach. She couldn't put them on the ground—what if Mrs. Betsy saw?—and she needed both hands to pull the rope. She turned toward the kitchen—but no, she was already here, so she turned back, face heating as a twitter of laughter rose behind her. *Land's—*

"Let me help," said a quiet voice. His freckled hands reached from a neatly tucked flannel shirt covering broad shoulders. The clean-shaven fellow smiled, from his freckled cheeks to the prettiest hazel eyes glinting with orange.

Oh, my lands. An animacambire. Animal changers weren't rare in the Farmlands, but she'd never met one this handsome or with such a musical accent. From his lean, muscular body and tawny hair glinting blue-gray, he had to be a bird. He was a head taller than she was—although most folks were, so he wasn't especially tall.

"Then you can ring the lunch bell?" He cupped one hand to the bowl, his warm fingers overlapping hers.

A shiver shot through her. Mary Clare pushed the bowl to him when what she really wanted was to open her Knack to learn if he was genuinely as nice as he appeared. She couldn't, and with her head muddled, she must be staring like a townie going into the Wildlands.

"Uh, thank you." She forced herself to turn and grasp the rope, cringing as hoots accompanied the peals. The ten rings for lunch gave her nerves time to settle. Those bloody farmhands acted like a herd of toddlers. She was new and had to take it until she had a position secured here. Then they'd get a piece of her mind.

When she turned back to collect her rolls, the fellow had carried the bowl to the back door.

Blocking the entrance, he faced the line of workers. "We'd heard the kitchen was short-staffed today, so you lot will count to one hundred, *slowly*, before you put on your best manners and *walk* into the dining room and collect your plates in a manner befitting Wellspring. Because if you're hungry now, think how much hungrier you'll be when dinner is late because you've flustered this new staffer and she's decided to throw in her apron and leave our overworked cook with no help."

Folks shuffled, and someone called, "Sorry, miss." Others echoed the apology.

That's all it took? Then standing up to these workers would be the same as putting Pa's hired hands in place. Times fifteen, but she could do it. Mary Clare raised her chin and surveyed the growing line. She said, "Accepted," and gave them a firm nod before striding to the 'cambire fellow and taking back her bowl with a grateful smile.

He opened the door for her. Mary Clare marched inside, and he easily caught up, their footsteps echoing down the dim back hallway. Was all that just an excuse to be first in line?

When they turned left into the quiet dining room, he asked, "You must be a sister to Mary Beth."

Everyone could tell the freckled, strawberry-blondes were sisters, even when they weren't side by side. "Mary Clare," she answered as she slid the bowl onto the sideboard with the other food. "I've helped out before. Usually during the harvest."

"Mary Clare," he repeated. "Then I would've been far too tired to notice. I was a day guard until a month ago."

"And now?"

"Mary Clare?" Mrs. Betsy called, startling her. The stout cook stood in the kitchen doorway, a bowl of orange mash held against her flowered apron. "This food does not deliver itself, duck."

Mary Clare darted over and took the warm bowl. *Land's sake, I canna make the cook angry, or this won't become permanent.* She dared not risk talking more, but she didn't even know his name!

"Sorry for the delay, ma'am," the fellow said to Mrs. Betsy. "Some of the new hires forgot Wellspring operates on manners. They're pausing outside to remember. Can I help?"

Mrs. Betsy *tsked*. "Please take these..." Her voice muffled as she turned to the table they used for staging the serving dishes. "You're a good lad, Rivley."

Rivley. His name was Rivley.

AFTER COLLECTING HIS FOOD, Rivley scanned for a place at the long dining room table. The cook's assistant wouldn't be sitting down to lunch. Only at dinner, which was served family style, did the kitchen staff sit. Not that he would sit with her then—they always sat at the end closest to the kitchen. But he could be early and select a nearby chair to overhear anything she said, even if he didn't speak with her again. He rubbed his growling stomach.

His fingers grazed the metal talisman underneath his waistband. What was he thinking? He was in the same situation he'd been in since leaving Rockbridge—the situation *they* were in. A clicking rose in Rivley's throat, and he quickly squelched his irritation. He and his best friend, Daeryn Darkcoat, shared the blame for the accident in which a teammate had died. The gildan enchantment the Elders had imposed bound them together and limited their social privileges—like the taking of life mates. Yet, a year and a half later, Daeryn still refused to address the lessons to learn what they'd done wrong so they could resolve the bond. Rivley was starting to question when Dae would learn to live with the grief.

So what was the point in courting someone?

Chairs scraped across the slate floor as the hungry growers seated themselves. Rivley carried his meal to a spot with a view of the kitchen door and sat. He didn't know Mary Clare at all. Why push Daeryn when it might be for naught and cause a rift?

Within seconds, Mary Clare emerged, said, "Excuse me," and added rolls to the bowl, as if shoving aside men twice her size was a daily occurrence.

"Can you sneak me out some cake?" a bloke asked her.

Mary Clare laughed and walked away, leaving the grumbly worker to stalk back to his chair.

Rivley found himself grinning at the redhead's alpha manner.

"What has you smiling for once?" asked Famil, who led the day guard team. She scooted into the next chair and began eating.

Neck heating, Rivley ducked his chin and spooned up squash. "I smile," he muttered.

Famil laughed softly. "You are the most solemn person I know. Good for a guard. Well, if we were guarding people. Half the staff are afraid to approach you." When he didn't respond, she added, "Fancy a mating dance with that little Knack-bearer?"

Heck, secrets didn't last long in this community. Even when there wasn't anything to keep secret. Famil, twice his twenty years, probably had a better sense than he would. "You think she's a Knack-bearer?"

"Hmm? Let me take another look." When Mary Clare re-entered, Famil narrowed her eyes. Their shape changed slightly, bringing her 'cambire's golden eagle sight into play.

He should learn this trick.

"Not a 'cambire, that's for sure. She's sisters with the other redheads who work here, right?"

There were more than one?

"Like them, could be a grower Knack or a human," Famil continued. "It doesn't always pass down."

Rivley nodded. He couldn't be interested. Not until he and Daeryn resolved their gildan.

Famil said goodbye, carried her dishes to the serving tray and intercepted Mr. Hortens. They had a word, then the head grower walked in Rivley's direction. He hurriedly chased his last beans before the man arrived.

"Will those spiders be done soon?"

Rivley wiped his mouth and rose. "They're done now, sir. However, I'd like to review operations with their operators. Could they stop by?"

Mr. Hortens eyed him.

By the Creator, had he made a mistake only hours into his responsibility? He started to add Master Brightwell had requested it when Mr. Hortens spoke.

"Five of the new hires continue to have operations issues

with their spiders. All would benefit from another review, and perhaps coming from a mechanic, it will make a stronger point. Rather than carting in the three other machines, are you willing to ride out and conduct the training on the hillsides?"

"Sure. If you have an available wagon, I'll load the spiders and head over."

That pleased Mr. Hortens, which pleased Rivley. In another hour, he could start that inventory.

Out in the field, a grower rushed to catch a machine at the end of a tilled row, and Rivley spotted the problem: They weren't guiding the machines far enough onto the roadbeds to make their turns before heading into the next row.

As he instructed Mr. Hortens' five growers, several others collected at the edges. Fine, training for more growers meant fewer repairs. After each executed proper turns, Rivley suggested they switch to walking on the downhill side to avoid bumping the machine.

Mr. Hortens clapped his hands for attention. "We have four hours to finish the fertilization before planting the peas. If he has the time, perhaps Mr. Slipwing can circulate and check each machine *while it is in operation.*"

Many scattered, but two young women approached and asked him to inspect their machines' joints, but then asked for his shop hours…unnecessary information.

Now, if it'd been Mary Clare asking…

CHAPTER 3

A knock came at the workshop door, followed by the squeal of metal wheels rolling on their track.

What now? A brisk draft circled Rivley's body, but he didn't turn from tightening the housing screws on his fifth repair of the day. "If your machine is even halfway operating, please return it to the equipment shed and take it out in the morning. The *repairs*"—he spat the word—"ahead of yours will take until afternoon."

A chuckle answered his order—a familiar one. Rivley leaned his head to the machine's cool metal. "Thank the Creator," he muttered, then louder, "Quick, close the door."

It squeaked again, and Daeryn Darkcoat tread over, flannel shirt barely tucked into his trousers, but his unruly dark hair was brushed and brown cheeks freshly shaved for his night's work. "I don't even have to ask. At dinner, the female growers were all a-twitter at having the opportunity to have a word with you."

"Argh!" Rivley threw down his grease rag. "They claim *something* is wrong with their spiders. Several had dirt in the joints, but not compacted like the fallen ones. Two had lost screws on the housing. One had a leg disconnected."

"You have to tell Hortens the damage was intentional."

Rivley rose. "And sound like I canna handle the workshop?"

"Then call out to them what you said to me."

"I have. Turned away the last three."

Daeryn swept his hand toward the five machines in line and laughed. "Does appear you should have caught on sooner. Just thought I'd pass on the chatter. Do yourself a favor and get dinner before it's cold."

"I want these two done before I head to bed."

Daeryn walked to the door. "You're taking this too seriously. Don't you think of anything besides mechanics these days?"

"Not if I want my own shop…" Well, there was something. "Did that new kitchen helper survive the day?"

"The redhead? Yep, she was eating with her sister. Cute—oh no." Daeryn waved his hands. "Please don't say it."

Rivley crossed his arms. "Haven't said a thing."

Daeryn narrowed his eyes. "You haven't asked after a female since we left Rockbridge. But unlike those girls, this one isn't 'cambire."

"That matters because?"

Daeryn frowned, going all alpha…except for the telltale slide of his hand over his gildan talisman.

Rivley eyed him. "We're not returning to Rockbridge any time soon."

"Maybe not ever," Daeryn said quietly.

"Maybe not ever," Rivley repeated. "No decision yet."

"Unless you fall for a human."

Or a Knack-bearer, but neither would fit into life in the Black Mountains. Rivley tapped his belly. "We *won't* have a life waiting for us there. Unless you'll start work on this gildan."

Daeryn huffed. "Don't have time to argue. I have to begin my guard rotation, or Owen will be on my tail." He shoved open the door, letting in the cold. "At dinner, Hortens announced smudge duty, whatever that is. In particular, he called on the growers

whose machines are in repair. And the mechanic's assistant."
Then Daeryn banged the door closed, cutting off the draft.

Smudge duty?

FOLLOWING DINNER, Mary Clare cleaned the dishware and platters, then started on the roasting pan. Mrs. Betsy was ferrying leftovers to the icebox off the screened-in porch and speaking with someone.

Dinner had gone well…except Rivley never turned up. Good, because she hadn't been distracted by him. Bad, because she was dying to check if his hair was as blue as she'd thought. She sighed and scrubbed at the stubborn edge of browned grease.

Chilly air whooshed into the kitchen before Mrs. Betsy firmly closed the door. "Land's sake, I swear we've retreated to February." She *tsked* and set down the crock of butter and a bowl of eggs. "This isn't good." She took a large mixing bowl from where Mary Clare had stored it in the cupboard and retrieved the farm's bread pans.

"What's wrong?" Even as she asked, Mary Clare's thoughts raced back to breakfast and her family's concern about how cool it'd been overnight. Pa had said if the temperature dropped further, they'd need to put out the smudge pots for—

"The cherry blossoms," Mrs. Betsy said.

"Oh, dear. What is the temperature?" The smoking smudge pots would warm the undersides of the cherry trees to protect the blossoms from freezing.

"Down to five degrees Celsius already. Mr. Hortens will give it another hour before he decides."

A snort escaped Mary Clare before she thought to hold back her opinion.

Mrs. Betsy raised her white brows.

Darn it, now she'd ruined a perfectly good workday. Face

warming, she said, "I...uh, my pa will have the pots filled and my sisters setting them out. At five degrees, he wants to be prepared. But we only have six trees for family use. I'm sure it's a bigger decision on a large collective."

Mrs. Betsy's frown cleared. "Ach, true. Eight rows, Mistress Gere has—eighty trees. You're from a farming family, so you understand." Mrs. Betsy peered at her speculatively. "While you finish up, duck, I'll start an extra batch of bran breads. If tonight's temperatures plummet, it'll be as busy as daytime out there."

Right, just like at home when she and her sisters would bundle up and check the pots and fan the smoke with Pa. Coming in to Granny's sweet biscuits and hot chocolate always felt good. It'd been a few years since they'd had a freeze during blossom time, so now even Mary Frances was old enough to pitch in. She didn't need to rush home. "Can I help with anything?" she offered.

The back door creaked, and Rivley stepped in.

Mary Clare's heart began thumping. He closed the door, glanced at her and ran his fingers through tufted bluish hair. Her breath caught.

"Yes, duck?" Mrs. Betsy asked him.

"I, uh, Mr. Hortens sent me in. I missed dinner, and we're to work tonight."

"He's decided, then, has he? Of course you need food. Everyone will need food. Mary Clare, get this boy some food, whatever he wants." Mrs. Betsy plucked a plate from the stack and pointed toward the porch.

Mary Clare took it and cast a smile at Rivley. But he wasn't smiling, and she quickly looked down. What was wrong? Had she done...no, of course not. She hadn't even been around him. Had he heard something about her? Only her sisters knew her here. She approached the door, but he leaned forward, opened it and gestured her out. She all but brushed him, not intending to be that close, but they had no extra room, what with Mrs. Betsy's rocking chair at the woodstove.

Then a thread of doubt wafted off him.

No! Her Knack wards had come down! It'd been a long day, and she was tired… Understandable to her family, but forbidden to everyone else.

On the screened porch, she darted into the outdoor pantry. Plenty of time to reinforce her wards while he waited in the kitchen… Footsteps sounded behind her, and his pang of hunger gripped at her own gut and twisted.

"Shall I hold the plate?" He shifted from foot to foot.

"Uh, thanks." With a shiver—only half from the darned cold —Mary Clare pushed the plate to him. "Wait there," she ordered and moved two blessed steps away. His feelings dissipated. Opening the icebox door, she gripped the handle and pretended to look over the contents. She pulled at the magic in her. *Come on.* It moved sluggishly, like it knew she only half wanted it to. Yep, she'd love to know what this fellow felt about her, but he was a stranger, and no matter how nice he was, she couldn't pry.

After a moment, the magic wrapped completely around her, sealing off the outside. Her breath rushed out. *Thank the Creator.*

"I'm not particular," he said. "Those beans will be fine."

"Mrs. Betsy would have my head if you came in with just a plate of beans." Setting out several containers on the adjacent table, Mary Clare found the leftover chicken. She reached for a piece, then stopped. This wasn't family. She needed a serving fork and hadn't brought one, nor a spoon for vegetables. "I shouldn't be touching your food. I'll fetch a fork—"

His stomach growled. "Excuse me. Can I just take one while you…" When she offered, he plucked out a leg and immediately took a bite, closing his eyes to chew.

Mary Clare set down the dish and skirted around him. "Be right back."

By the time she returned, he'd eaten that piece and started on another. With the fork stuck in the meat in case he wanted more, she heaped beans and potatoes onto the plate he'd put on the table. "So, they're setting out the smudge pots soon?"

"Mr. Hortens is sending them 'round on a wagon for me to fill with Basin coal." He took another bite of chicken.

The way he said it… Something wasn't sitting right with him, which she could tell even without her Knack. "Surely there's enough?"

His alluring orange eyes darted aside. "Likely? Down in the Black Mountains, we don't use coal. I hope one of the growers knows how much it'll take."

Mary Clare nodded. "My sister knows…" What was she doing, volunteering Mary Beth? "*I* can show you how to fill the pots. Certain tools help so the goo doesn't get all over everything."

He frowned. "Goo?"

"*Basin* coal is unpredictable." She tilted a spoonful of squash. As it oozed onto his plate, she explained, "If you're lucky, it never gets looser than this and will stay on the shovel. But sometimes it turns with no warning and lands on the floor or, worse, your trousers and boots."

Grimacing, he shook his head. "I can't ask you to come out. It's dirty work."

She grinned. "It sure is. We heat with Basin coal at my family's place, so I've moved it lots. I know how to keep it from my clothes." Whether or not it dribbled over her best bib and brace, she'd get to spend more time with this polite fellow.

He nodded solemnly. "I'd appreciate the help, if Mrs. Betsy gives her permission. Give me five minutes?"

He carried his food into the kitchen, and Mary Clare thumped her forehead. Argh, this wasn't the Pemberton farm where everyone was expected to help.

❧

Minutes later, Rivley strode across the farmyard with Mary Clare, his belly now full and his head clearer. With her help, he wouldn't have to admit he couldn't deliver what Mr. Hortens wanted. He eyed the short female with a new appreciation. Never had she said to Mrs. Betsy he didn't know anything about Basin coal. Instead, she'd offered to help in the kitchen for the evening and asked for a ten-minute break, "For a bit of fresh air and physical movement helping Rivley fetch coal for the smudge pots."

Mrs. Betsy had *tutted* and proclaimed it a blessing not having the nasty stuff in the house any longer. As soon as he'd eaten, she'd shooed them out.

He led the way to the stall in the back of the workshop. There, on hooks above the coal, hung several buckets, a shovel and long-handled scoops made from metal cans, all stained with a tar-like substance.

Mary Clare banged together two larger scoops over a bucket. Pieces of coal pattered down, leaving the scoops clean. "The coal from last use rehardened. Let's see how the rest reacts tonight." She set the bucket close to the pile of black hunks and gestured for him to use the shovel he'd taken down.

He tried to push the shovel into the pile, but the metal *thunked* like he'd hit a rock. "It's a single lump."

She laughed. "For now. Hit it again from the top."

He did, and miraculously, a chunk broke off.

"Quick, shovel it into the bucket." She leaned forward and held a scoop between the pile and the bucket.

Not the easiest shoveling, but he'd try it her way before suggesting she move back.

The shovel slid under the lump, but as he swung, it melted like he'd lit a fire beneath it. "Whoa." He hesitated, and she caught the trail of liquid running off the blade.

"Go on," she ordered, startling him into action.

He dumped the mush into the bucket. "This will burn?"

She poured her liquid onto the top, and lumps formed again,

like the crystallization of sugar candy. "It will. Smoke, too. It's tricky filling the smudge pots. An ice pick is handy."

"We've got those."

They filled a bucket, and Mary Clare straightened. "The growers will need more than these four buckets to keep the smudge pots smoking all night."

Mr. Hortens had explained that. Apparently, Master Brightwell always helped monitor the smoking, and Hortens wanted Rivley to fill in. It seemed expected rather than a request. "Why don't they use deeper pots if they don't last all night?"

"A low level of lit coal produces more smoke when you get the vent adjusted just so." She indicated the first joint of her pointer finger. "About this much in the bottom. More, and they flame and waste coal."

Her small hands made a different measure than his, so he automatically put his palm to hers, lining up their fingers. His first joint extended beyond hers. Three-quarters? Half? As he held her hand, trying to determine a precise measure, her skin turned from warm to clammy. *Oh. I made her nervous? Was it a good nervous?*

"It's, uh, approximate," she mumbled, pulling away her hand. "Checking them overnight is an event for sure, but saving the blossoms is worth it for the cherries."

His mouth watered. "Last year was my first taste of these sweet Farmlands cherries. They let us day guards eat the topmost ones the growers missed." Would she know what he meant? How would she react?

Her nose wrinkled. "How did you get them if…*oh*."

"On the wing," he confirmed. "They're easy to spot from the air."

She laughed. "You should come around my family place to clean up. I've always hated that we canna get every last one."

Grinning, he eyed her. She *sounded* comfortable with the animal shifters, but how comfortable? "I might just do that."

"Is your bird form light enough not to break the branches?" she asked as they filled the buckets.

He'd brought up the subject of 'cambires, and the query flowed naturally, but he detected the real question: *What are you?*

"Yes." He let that sit for a moment, and she bit her lip. The "don't ask what you aren't told" policy was ingrained into Basin residents as fledglings, kits and toddlers. You didn't pry into others' Knacks.

"I'm a Eurasian sparrowhawk," he said quietly. "From the Black Mountains."

"Ah. Pretty plumage."

He wasn't sure how she knew, since sparrowhawks didn't frequent the Farmlands. He waited for her to volunteer her heritage, but Mary Clare busied herself with the buckets, moving the empty ones closer to the pile. Soon, they'd filled them, their opportunity for private conversation disappointingly over.

They carried the buckets outside. The wagon had arrived, with two of the grower females who'd brought in their spiders. They didn't look happy to see Mary Clare. But then, she wasn't happy to see them.

Rivley suppressed a grimace. This game had played out so many times in Rockbridge, usually with him enjoying it. Tonight, he wanted to shoo it away. He remembered his manners and introduced Mary Clare while she set her buckets on the wagon.

Mary Clare pulled over a smudge pot, dug a scoop into a bucket and showed him the now-liquid coal. "Get out several scoopfuls real quick. If it hardens—and it probably will—whack it with the ice pick or jostle the buckets again."

The growers watched as she filled five pots and he managed two before the coal solidified. She lowered her bucket, kicked it twice and filled three more before it hardened again. "Weren't there more scoops? Folks could help if you fetch them, Rivley."

She handed her scoop to the nearest grower. "I have to get back to the kitchen, but let me know if you need help later."

He watched her walk off.

One of the growers harrumphed. "She's bossy for kitchen help."

"She knows more than we do." The other grower banged the closest bucket and poured a measure of liquid into a smudge pot. "Come on, or Mr. Hortens will be here before we're done."

Each of those things was true, and somehow warmed Rivley's belly. He handed off his scoop. "I'll fetch more." What excuse could he use to call upon Mary Clare later?

CHAPTER 4

R ivley placed a smudge pot where Mr. Hortens directed, beneath cherry limbs laced high above their heads, each twig bearing white buds glowing in the setting sun. Then the head grower demonstrated how to light the coal and adjust the vent once it caught. Lighting the pots fell to Rivley and a team of three—all but one new at this—while the wagon moved on.

Rivley positioned the flint scraper so the sparks would fall onto the coal. The porridge-like substance caught, but the next pot held solid hunks and required more strikes. The third, a pot of liquid coal, flared a foot high, singeing the hairs on the back of Rivley's hand.

"Too much in that one," yelled Sticks. "Shut the vent, quick!"

He put it out, and Sticks came to inspect it. The wiry, midthirties grower grumbled. As Mary Clare had said, overfilled ones burned too hot.

With the coal presenting differently in every smudge pot, Rivley couldn't get a rhythm. But he learned to judge the state of the coal and how close to place his flint scraper. By the third flash of flames, he easily rolled away. Rising to his knees, he raked fingers through his hair, feeling feathers poking through.

At least in the fading light, the others couldn't see how much this rattled him.

The youngest grower howled and fell back, shaking her hand.

"Iris, are you all right?" yelled another grower as three of them ran over.

"No," the teen cried. "I'm burned, and I canna tell how badly."

"This is horrible!" the other female groused. "The experienced staff should be out here, but instead, they get the night off so they'll be fresh for the morning planting."

"You will have the day to sleep," Sticks said. "This is how you gain experience, and if we have another freezing night, it'll go all the faster."

"I'll accompany her in," Rivley said, "and fetch a bucket for extra coal." He clasped Iris' elbow and walked her to the wagon road between the trees. She didn't protest as she cradled her hand.

A four-legged silhouette bounded toward them—Daeryn had heard Iris' cry.

"She needs to see the healer," Rivley called to the polecat. "Can you lead us down the quickest path?"

With a yip, the weasel-like figure leaped toward the trees and trotted forward, checking they were following. Rivley increased their pace, weaving between the branches behind Dae. Within minutes, he ushered Iris into the back hall of the farmhouse, called for the healer and delivered Iris to her.

He could collect the refuse bucket near the workshop door, but Mary Clare's offer of help echoed in his head. She knew what to do, if only Mrs. Betsy would agree.

The dining room glowed with light. Hot kettles lined the sideboard, and the tray of butter and jams sat at the ready. The scents of cinnamon and sugar wafted from the kitchen, followed by the sweet aroma of berries as he approached the doorway. Mouth watering, he was blocked by a serving table lined with rows of muffins, the pink ones reminding him of the cherry trees he had to get back to.

"Rivley, hello," Mary Clare called, quickening his heartbeats. She held a muffin tin filled with batter. Opening the oven, she bent to put in the tray.

Oh, drat. She was busy.

"What can we get you, duck?" Mrs. Betsy approached the opposite side of the table. "We have meats, too, and cheese with bread if you need to keep moving." She gestured to the stacked napkins.

"Thank you." He took a pink muffin, which was indeed studded with canned cherries. "Actually, Iris was burned in a flare—"

"No!" exclaimed Mary Clare, coming up behind the cook.

"—which wouldn't have happened if more growers knew what to do. Mary Clare knows. Could you spare her to help us light the pots? An hour, maybe?"

Mary Clare opened her mouth, then closed it again and looked over at the cook.

Rivley held his lips in a firm line, not cracking a smile or daring to glance her way again. Great Creator, this female was used to doing things her way, but was adapting quickly to Wellspring's ways.

"Poor little Iris." Mrs. Betsy shook her head. "Of course." She turned Mary Clare by the shoulders, like she wouldn't have gone on her own. "Fetch your jacket, duck. I can manage on my own for an hour."

While Mary Clare put on her coat and scarf, he bit into his muffin. It was good, a new flavor that had to be Mary Clare's recipe.

Outside, he asked her, "Have you been baking long?"

"All my life. I love it, especially experimenting with flavors and seasonings for vegetables and meats. Most places have their signature tastes already established, but I've created some 'specials' at the hotel in Chapel Hollow."

They'd crossed the farmyard and passed the bunkhouse, her shorter legs keeping up with his pace. Should he take her elbow to guide her on the shortcut through the fruit trees? Her hand? Or would the confident female think he viewed her as weak? Rivley had interacted with alpha females in Rockbridge who would scoff at such a gesture, but with a human, this could go either way.

Beyond the greenhouse, Daeryn, in his polecat form, cleared the orchard grass in a leap.

With a hiss of breath, Mary Clare stumbled and pressed against Rivley. "What—*who*… Is that a guard?"

Automatically, his arm went around her shoulders. "That's Daeryn Darkcoat, a friend of mine. A European polecat."

"He's also from the Black Mountains?" She leaned into Rivley's side.

His breath hitched. "Ah—*yes*. A common 'cambire."

Daeryn paused before them, a cock of his head pinging awareness in Rivley.

He dropped his arm so only his fingers pressed the small of Mary Clare's back, a touch Daeryn wouldn't see. "He'll lead us on the quickest path to the teams. Thanks, Dae," he added.

Daeryn pivoted and leaped.

As they walked, Mary Clare's shoulder bumped Rivley while crossing the rough ground, so he clasped her elbow. She didn't pull away.

It took every ounce of strength Mary Clare had not to lean into Rivley again. He smelled like a breeze on an autumn day, reminding her of crinkling leaves. And he was nicely warm. She'd heard 'cambires had a higher body heat than Knacks or humans, but hadn't thought of bird shifters as being especially warm, compared to furry ones, like wolves.

She wished he'd hold her hand, rather than her elbow in such a formal posture. But he was polite, much more polite than some of her past suitors.

Rivley's friend kept looking back. She knew enough to know 'cambire hearing was sharp, and she couldn't ask, not while the polecat led them. Surely Daeryn heard their feet rustling the dried grass, so his curiosity gave her the feeling her sisters did when they were inspecting a boy. Had Rivley said something about her to him?

The scent of coal smoke grew stronger, then in the next orchard row, a fire flared, and voices rose.

"Land's sake!" She ran forward, following...er, the *growing* figure. The polecat rose on two legs as he shifted. Rivley sprinted past her, and they raced toward a patch of flaming grass.

Someone was scooping dirt onto the flames, and Daeryn, naked, joined him. Rivley whipped off his leather apron and dropped it over the high flames. He jumped onto it, stomping with his boots. A few flames licked at the edges, which a grower squelched with her boots, but the tilted smudge pot still flamed, its liquid coal streaming out.

Mary Clare darted to the pot, cursing she didn't have the metal poker Pa insisted they carry. She hitched up her trouser leg and kicked the thing over until it was upside down. Most of the flames extinguished when the opening hit the ground, then Rivley threw his apron over it.

The reek of charred grass surrounded them. Coughing, they moved away. Rivley pulled his shirt over his head and gave it to Daeryn, who yanked it on. The tails barely covered his nakedness.

Mary Clare's breathing, ragged from running and the excitement, had evened out but hitched again. Rivley's chest—*wow*. His beautifully sculpted muscles begged to be explored—argh, what was she thinking? Looking around, she asked, "What happened?"

The grower shook her head. "One flamed when I lit it. I jumped back and knocked over another."

"Are you all right?" Rivley asked, and she nodded.

Was he this nice to everyone? If so, then it probably meant nothing when he'd held her arm. Disappointment flooding her, Mary Clare flipped over Rivley's apron and righted the pot with her boot toe.

Sticks shone his lantern over it. The remaining coal had solidified into a cake and stuck out of the vent.

She broke it off using Rivley's flint sparker and prodded it into the hot metal pot.

"With the fire out, I'll return to my rounds," Daeryn said.

Rivley followed him a few steps, their voices a murmur. Trying to ignore them, Mary Clare showed the growers where the coal level should be and checked the other pots with them. By the time she demonstrated lighting one, Rivley returned—his shirt on, darn it—with the bucket he'd dropped.

After adjusting the coal levels and lighting these, the team moved to the next tree. Mary Clare stayed with the grower who'd started the fire until her hands no longer shook, then hung back while she lit the next.

Rivley came up beside her. "How's she doing?"

"Much better. How are you?"

He hefted the bucket. "Half are too full. Those growers helping me didn't follow your instruction, and I didn't check their work. Sticks said once the workers on the wagon finish putting out the pots, they'll start lighting from the other end."

The steam tractor chugged along several orchard rows away. "Ohhh, someone should tell them."

He nodded. "Would you come with me?" When she nodded, he called to Sticks, and they set off.

As they hurried, avoiding the low-hanging limbs was difficult. One snagged her hat, and another jabbed her shoulder. "Oof!"

Rivley waited for her, holding up a limb before the grassy road. When they entered another row, she reached for the bucket.

"Let me carry it while you save our heads."

He handed it over and held out a curved arm. "If you're right beside me, we can move faster. May I?"

Put his arm around her? She grinned. "Yes." That might have come out too enthusiastically, but who cared?

They wove between the limbs, Mary Clare tucked against his warm chest, the scent of fall leaves filling her nose. He seemed to grab branches from nowhere and lift them aside with one long arm.

"Do all 'cambires have good night eyesight?" she asked.

He made a sound that sounded like a squelched laugh. "Sorry, just thinking how Daeryn would howl over that one. My eyesight is terrible at night, likely no better than yours."

"Then how are you...?"

He shrugged against her. "I feel a branch coming and know how to avoid it."

They emerged onto the road and ducked into the last row. Across it, the tractor rumbled loudly, the moving lantern lights outlining the folks carrying them. "It's a bird thing?"

His hold on her loosened. "I suppose, from flying between trees. I hadn't thought of it before." One tree away, the workers hadn't seen them yet. Rivley dropped his arm. "'Cambires are different in many ways from...humans."

From you. Land's sake, this was going downhill, as Granny would say. Mary Clare didn't want it to.

He reached for the bucket.

Instead of releasing it, she stepped closer and looked up at him. "I come from a family of Knack-bearers. Most of us. We embrace different, because we are, too. You can't live in a long-time market town like Chapel Hollow and not. Your differences are good."

Slowly, his cheeks lifted in a smile, and she smiled back. He leaned toward her, head tilting as if he was moving in for a kiss. Then his gaze shifted toward the tractor.

A wince of disappointment froze her. The growers couldn't see. Or was he worried what *she* thought? One way to solve that.

She tugged the bucket handle. He followed it, and she clutched his jacket collar to lower his head while she went onto tiptoes. Her lips brushed his cheek, not really where she was aiming, but that should relay the message.

She parted, but he didn't move…her hand still held his collar. Oh. She released him, but his head descended again, and this time, his lips met hers.

Rivley tasted sweet—her muffins, she realized—and the wind, if that had a taste. Also, like trees in the breeze and faraway mountaintops and…wild mint.

Mary Clare shivered, and Rivley lifted his head from the kiss, his gaze fixed on her, his hand cupping her elbow as she lowered onto her heels.

"All right?" he whispered in his endearing accent.

"Oh, yes," she gushed, and her cheeks heated at how giddy she must sound. Yet, she couldn't stop grinning.

He flashed a crooked grin and nodded toward a small commotion she hadn't noticed. "We best…"

Someone cursed, and in unison Mary Clare and Rivley paced toward the growers. While he asked what'd happened, she checked the smudge pot, emptied a third of it into the bucket Rivley held and demonstrated how to light the proper amount. She said nothing, letting him give the instructions and answer questions.

Just kissing Rivley had been like an adventure. So different than her previous short-time beau she couldn't even compare. With this gentle 'cambire, she could just erase that memory and renew her dreams. She loved her family and routine at home, but she'd always wanted to meet someone who would be a partner in adventure.

~

Rivley forced himself to pay attention to the growers. He wasn't angry when they admitted they'd added more coal to avoid having to do refills. Their friend's burn topped any punishment his words could dole out, so he took their apology and mindful attention to Mary Clare's demonstrations as a lesson learned.

The kiss with Mary Clare had felt like flying, that lifting mindlessness of just sensing the currents and letting them take him. He glanced at the short redhead bundled in her woolen jacket. Why was she so quiet now? Not a bad quiet. She'd liked their kiss. She'd started it after all, but that little peck had only made him curious. Yes, she knew how to kiss…and maybe more.

They worked through additional pots to verify these growers knew the correct coal levels. But he wanted to walk into the dark with Mary Clare. Every time he came close to her, his excitement built. Finally, she murmured apologetically that she should return to the kitchen. Yet, she slipped her hand into his as they walked the long way down the row to the farm road.

They stopped in the shadows of the bunkhouse, out of sight of the farmhouse and a few workers crossing the yard. He put his arms around her, and in seconds, their lips met. Opened. His tongue teased over hers, which traced his lips before returning to his. Like the burst of a tail wind, their lips and tongues worked in a frenzy, and he clung to her like the drop would kill him.

At last, he parted for a breath. "It's so…exciting," he murmured. "I haven't felt this way in a long time." He should tell her why he hadn't courted anyone in two years, about the gildan. Why this could go only so far… *What am I thinking? It's a kiss, not a life-mate commitment.*

Mary Clare looked up at him with unfocused eyes. "What? Oh—" She bit her lip and pressed fingers to her forehead.

Something was wrong. He could see it in her face, how her manner had changed… She felt stiff against him now. He should let her go, but he didn't want to. She wasn't pulling away. "Change your mind about kissing?" he asked, trying to do so lightly.

"Not that." She stroked his shoulder. "That was the most wonderful kiss. I'd love to continue, but I'm on trial for this job, and Mrs. Betsy must expect me. I can't bungle this."

"Can I see you later?" he blurted, surprising himself. "If you want to…"

"I do," she said quickly.

"I'd like to tell you…uh, trade more about ourselves. In the past, I grew up in the same shire as those I've courted." Great Creator, did he just say *courted*?

Stepping back, she tossed him a wry smile and ran her hands down her trousers. "I never have—known the fellow well, I mean. I've courted. Talking would be good, but…" She looked around. "I wouldn't know where to find you."

CHAPTER 5

Mary Clare hedged her wording, giving Rivley a chance to back out. She'd let her Knack sway him. That was as dangerous as telling him about it.

She pressed her hand to her head again, assuring herself her wards were up. These last minutes, he'd been free from her sway. Seeing her again was his idea. She was sure…she thought. With a Knack like hers, she didn't have a lot of practice reading facial expressions.

"I'll come by the kitchen," Rivley said.

She stopped a flurry of words from rushing out. *I must calm down and focus on doing my job well.* "Sorry if I can't leave. I don't know Mrs. Betsy's plans for tonight."

The sooner she walked across the farmyard and into the kitchen, the sooner she would be to finishing work and seeing Rivley again. And—darn it—she needed the time alone to reconstruct *solid* walls for their next kiss. *Exciting*, he'd said. Well, she'd certainly felt excited.

He twined his slender fingers with hers and squeezed as they walked.

She squeezed back. *I promise, I won't let that happen again.* She had to let him have his feelings alone to know what he truly felt about her, not her projected feelings…unlike her last beau.

At the door, she climbed the steps so she wouldn't hug him again and, with a last squeeze of his hand, said good-bye. He smiled and hurried off.

Mrs. Betsy, at the far end of the warm kitchen speaking with several growers, hadn't heard her enter. Mary Clare hung her outer things and began washing dishes.

The last time she hadn't been careful—with a fellow she'd met at Market Day. He was her age and cute, and as Granny said, she'd pinned her feelings on her sleeve. *Her Knack.* For weeks, he'd bought sweets while she worked at Mrs. Ruby's, and on her breaks, they'd kiss and such in the alley. Then he'd go back to his farm, hours distant from Chapel Hollow.

Her older sisters had told her all about the next level of a relationship, which she'd already known from growing up on a farm. She'd thought she was ready, but that first time, her Knack had run rampant, and so had his excitement. He'd been too rough, they'd fought, and when she'd returned, weepy, her sisters had gotten the secret out without much prodding. They'd told Ma, who'd insisted her Knack be warded, which Mary Clare had already realized. Thereafter, the fellow hadn't been interested, proving how dangerous her *talent* could be.

An hour later, Mary Clare was washing dishes again. Farmworkers came and went, none of them Rivley, so she stopped looking up until a familiar voice asked for milk. Mary Clare whirled around, and Mary Beth grinned at her across the room.

"Will you be ready to go soon? I could walk you home before my shift starts." She lowered her voice. "And hear why you're still here on your first day."

Mary Clare glanced at the clock. Its hands pointed nearly straight up.

Also seeing the time, Mrs. Betsy *tsked.* "You should go, duck. Though your help has made my evening easy. One of the night guards will walk you two."

Or Rivley could walk her out...though the path to their family farm led opposite the cherry trees and his work. Which must be busy, because he hadn't been in again. She stopped a sigh from slipping out. There would be time to see him and make a connection, even if she didn't get the position here. She eyed her sister. "Or I could sleep in your bed since you'll be working, and I would be early to help at breakfast before I leave for the hotel." She'd already told Mrs. Betsy about her standing Wednesday lunch special. The meal had been announced, so Mrs. Betsy said Mary Delia could fill in.

Mary Beth and Mrs. Betsy both eyed her, then each other.

"All right," Mary Beth said. "I'll let you in our entrance."

Complex Knack protections permitted only those her sisters chose into their room. But if she left the kitchen, and Rivley came... Mary Clare chewed on her lip.

"I'd be happy for your help in the morning, duck," Mrs. Betsy said. "It'll be an off-schedule day with many arriving late for breakfast."

"I'd love to help," Mary Clare said automatically, and she meant it. She fetched her coat. As soon as they were outside, she pulled her sister beneath the shadows of a walnut tree in the farmyard's circular drive. "Do you know a fellow named Rivley?"

The porch light lit Mary Beth's wicked grin. "Sooo? You've met Rivley?"

"Just tell me what you know about him."

She crossed her arms. "You saw him in the dining room? Or you tried talking to him?"

"We've chatted." Mary Clare didn't want to say she *liked him* until she'd learned more.

"Wait. He *talked* to you?"

Mary Clare started to huff, then stopped. The way Mary Beth said that... Rivley didn't talk to anyone? She shivered at the news. *Maybe he does really like me.*

Her sister unfolded her arms and patted her shoulder. "After the last fellow, I don't blame you for asking. He was—"

"Please!" Mary Clare pressed her temples. "Don't mention that louse."

Mary Beth sighed sympathetically. "None of the female staff have gotten to know Rivley, but everyone wants to. He fixed my spider machine weeks ago, and I was considering him—"

"No." Mary Clare gripped her arm. "You're not, or you'd already have tried."

Mary Beth blew out a breath. "I did try and got nowhere. He's quiet, though I wouldn't say shy. Really quiet. I can tell he's gentle by the way he cares for the machines."

Mary Clare frowned. "Are you saying he'll treat me like a machine?"

"Yes. No. I mean, he's careful with his tools, never says a mean word even when you've missed an oil change. Sheesh, if you can get him to talk to you, you're lucky."

A smile crawled over Mary Clare's face before she could stop it.

Mary Beth squeaked and shook her shoulder. "Ah, that's wonderful. Now if we could get you hired here full time…"

"Exactly. Take me to your room."

Minutes later, Mary Beth had shared the magical warding, and the sisters parted. Too restless and not wanting to wake Mary Alice, Mary Clare went to the bunkhouse's outer door. She checked her wards while scanning the farmyard. *Rivley has to be out there still. If I find him, we could have that talk…or something.*

She'd make enemies if she waltzed in and snatched up a sought-after fellow. Her experience with males was limited, but with six sisters, she knew all about jealousy. Especially having an emotional Knack. Rivley was handsome and nice. And so serious.

A low whistle sounded.

She looked around, gripping the door handle. A figure

hurried across the farmyard. She released the latch along with a breath as an apron flapped around his long legs. Rivley.

"Was that whistle you?" she asked as he approached.

He nodded, and a nervous laugh escaped her.

"Do you need help?" she asked.

"The early team is training the new shift. I'd like you to make sure they have things correct."

Well, with Mary Beth working, they would have them correct, but she didn't need to tell Rivley that. Mary Clare smiled. They'd get in that talk.

He led the way to the mechanic's workshop, where four buckets waited. "If you don't mind, we can take these along."

Now, smoke hung underneath the trees in a thick fog, the air warm. Out of habit, Mary Clare took Rivley's lantern and checked the level of a pot cranking out smoke.

"Three-quarters of an hour left before it needs refilling."

He looked into it. "Seriously? You can tell to that precise a time?"

She shrugged. "To an hour, but you don't want them going out, so best to be early. Were these the first put out?"

"From this end, yes." They left two buckets at the tree.

She heard Mary Beth directing folks before they reached the group's lantern glows. "My sister will keep these folks on track." Mary Clare clasped Rivley's elbow. "Let's find the other team."

With a nod, Rivley pivoted in the roadway, put an arm around her shoulders and led them between trees.

His arm is only to guide me. They wove through rows, spied lanterns and met with the new team, some only barely awake.

She went over lighting and refilling the pots and helped this team, while Rivley ferried coal. In an hour, he found her again. A warm fuzziness filled her as they surveyed the smoke wafting through the branches and the bobbing lanterns' blurry glows.

"Mr. Hortens is pleased this is running so smoothly. I told him you've been advising us."

"You did? He doesn't even know me."

Rivley laughed. "He knows Mary Beth and wishes she'd been on the first shift. Your sister set him straight that you're more than capable."

"That's Mary Beth," she said. "Always ready to speak her mind." Land's sake, Mary Beth wouldn't have said anything to Rivley about Mary Clare's interest, would she?

"He'd like to sleep a few hours and return when it'll be the coldest. I told him I could manage the coal ferrying and refilling if you and your sister were available for troubleshooting." Rivley's eyebrows rose.

It'd mean she'd be awake all night before working breakfast here, Mrs. Ruby's for lunch and then returning in the late afternoon. Mary Clare bit her lip. Missing sleep sounded awful, but Rivley looked so hopeful…

"I know it's a lot to ask when you aren't even on staff—"

"I can do it," she said quickly. The meal at Mrs. Ruby's was planned, a dish she could cook in her sleep, or without any.

Once they'd refilled the buckets, both leaned in to pick them up at the same time, cheeks brushing.

Mary Clare froze. *Will he kiss me?* Desire swelled in her…

In a split second, Rivley ducked. His lips molded smoothly to hers, and her heart leaped.

That taste of the wild wind again—*oh, my!* She nibbled his bottom lip and kissed him back. They straightened, buckets forgotten, hands on each other instead. Her head muddled.

He was so perfect. To fall for a fellow so quickly—

Her Knack—she caught it just as the wards slipped.

RIVLEY'S HEARTBEATS SPED. She was smart and fun. Easy to talk to. At Mary Clare's willingness, he deepened the kiss. They kissed until they were as breathless as racing on the wing between tree branches and broke apart.

Panting, she touched her head.

He'd asked before, and she'd brushed it off, so he simply put an arm around her and nudged her closer. She hugged him. A chucking rose in his chest, an involuntary avian show of satisfaction. He squelched it. Fine, she made him happy, but Great Creator, what would she think of his bird habits?

To cover it, he stroked her chin and lifted it to kiss her again, which she returned eagerly. All right, she'd said she didn't mind 'cambires, so he'd continue being friendly.

They were later getting back to the cherry rows than he'd planned. No one noticed, because he'd been hiking all through the trees in the dark. They refilled pots, checked with team leaders, then returned to the workshop to reload the coal buckets. And kiss again.

This time with more touching.

After dropping off two buckets, they strolled across the rows with their fingers entwined, a haze of pleasure filling his head… until they crossed paths with a certain polecat guard. They dropped hands immediately—as much her idea as his, it seemed.

Daeryn went on his way, but heck, the mere sight of his best friend rocked Rivley back on his heels. He hadn't talked to Mary Clare like he'd promised himself he would. She'd hinted she was a Knack-bearer, so kissing wasn't too serious. Not enough to confess his gildan bond.

Mary Clare stiffened when he clasped her hand again. "I like you, Rivley, but I'm not ready to let anyone else know we're… this." She raised their linked hands.

"Agreed. I don't care for gossip, and"—he sighed—"there will be gossip. Are you ready for that?"

She grinned. "I can take it. Six sisters. But I need to secure the kitchen position. If I don't, then we can…"

His belly dropped. *Not* go their separate ways. "Decide then? You don't need to live here for us to see each other."

"I want this position."

He nodded. "It's only been a year and a half since Daeryn

and I arrived in the Farmlands looking for work, and I recall the feeling."

A team's lanterns came into sight, and they stopped in the dark. "You don't feel this is only my idea?" she asked.

"What? No, I returned to fetch you, hoping."

"*Before* you whistled?"

What was she getting at? Should he admit it? "Definitely before."

She broke into a broad smile. "Good." The smile faded, and she pressed her head again. "I sometimes want things so much I convince others it's the thing to do."

They'd just met, but she clearly felt the same about not keeping secrets. "I like you, too, but I have to tell you—"

Her bucket clunked to the ground, her arms wrapped him, and her lips demanded he kiss her. His bucket followed, and they clung together, tongues feverishly exploring.

He parted from her to whisper, "Don't worry. I want this, too. Maybe more."

She laughed. "Really?" Her hand slid to his rear and pulled him closer.

His breath caught. "Yes," he rasped.

"Hello?" someone called. "Rivley, are you there? We've a smudge pot out."

"Oh, lands!" Mary Clare flung herself back. "My sister."

He snatched up the buckets and strode forward, breathing deeply to clear his head. Mary Clare followed a few paces behind. After they refilled the pot, someone reported another sputtering.

Mary Clare returned from checking around the next tree. "A number of these are low and should be filled now."

She and Mary Beth frowned at each other, then at two growers. One female kicked at the ground. "We didn't want to be burned like Iris, so we kept the coal level low."

"Eyeball the measure," Mary Beth said. "The depth you'd plant squash seed."

The growers eyed Rivley instead. The same looks as when the females brought in their purposefully damaged spider machines. Sheepish. *Great Creator.* He knew what this was about. But accusing them aloud of doing this to get his attention sounded like putting on airs.

Mary Beth looked between them and him, then snapped her fingers. "See here. We are *not* compromising the cherry crop so new workers can get a closer look at the cute mechanic's assistant. These trees are our responsibility, not his."

Rivley's ears burned while the females scampered to fill their smudge pots.

"Mary Clare, check the other team's pots." Mary Beth jabbed a finger. "Tell them I sent you. I'll survey my rows, then talk to the other leader about this...situation." For the first time, she glanced at Rivley. "Sorry to call them out in front of you, but I promise I'll put a stop to these antics. Could you bring more coal?"

"I'll bring the wheelbarrow." He handed the lantern to Mary Clare.

Mary Beth took the bucket from him, but as she marched away, Mary Clare caught her arm and leaned in to whisper.

Rivley turned and walked off. They'd agreed to keep things secret. So what could she be telling her sister?

CHAPTER 6

Mary Clare didn't want to cross Mary Beth while she was this far up on her high horse. But she had to start out at Wellspring like she'd be here permanently, and that meant working *alongside* her sister. Mary Clare hissed, "Don't boss me around like we're at home."

"I-I'm sorry," Mary Beth whispered, her hands fisted as they walked on. "I forgot. I was just so angry to see them gawking at Rivley."

Anger wasn't what Mary Clare had felt, but she held her tongue. Thank goodness her sister had said what she couldn't, but now that she and Rivley had an agreement, she was sticking to it. She smacked Mary Beth's arm. "You sounded like Pa back there. No nonsense."

Mary Beth grunted. "I don't want this crop lost on my watch."

"Nope, and I'll help." She cut beneath the trees to find the other team.

Two growers had skimped on coal, causing four pots to go out. When Mary Clare's coal was gone, Sticks sent those folks back with her to fetch additional buckets from the greenhouse and shovel more coal. To her amusement, when they met

Rivley returning with the wheelbarrow, they didn't meet his gaze.

Once back in the orchard, Mary Beth wasn't around, so Mary Clare answered questions, moving from smoky tree to smoky tree. The air brushing her cheeks felt warm, definitely above freezing.

Rivley found her with a team. "Mary Beth and Sticks have decided the growers will ferry coal and asked us to check the pot levels. Will you?"

Mary Beth is handing me time alone with Rivley? Then…she wasn't pursuing him. "Where should we start?"

Rivley smiled, and her head muddled with happiness. He'd meant it earlier when he said he'd hoped she'd come out with him.

Now, she needed to keep her wits about her—and her Knack warded.

RIVLEY LED THE WAY TO STICKS' rows in the smoky half darkness. After they'd walked out of earshot, he clasped Mary Clare's elbow. With no more than that, they were in each other's arms. The kiss was long and thorough. He was ready for more, but at a rustling of footsteps, he lay a finger across her lips.

"Someone is coming."

She cocked her head. "I don't hear anyone."

"Trust me. I do." He tapped his ear.

They strode beneath the tree and separated to check the pots, just before two growers ducked in from the other side.

After a brief conversation, they started down the row.

"My eyesight's excellent, but not in the dark." He held his breath.

"That's why you were a day guard," she said matter-of-factly.

His heart raced as he slid his hand into hers. This was going well. He'd tell her more about guarding at Rockbridge and lead up to the gildan. Yet, when they escaped into darkness, Mary Clare cuddled into him. Sneaking kisses between trees grew only more exciting. Even dropping hands when anyone approached, they became more familiar over the cold hours. When Mr. Hortens joined them for the coldest hour before dawn, Rivley had to bite his tongue. *Why now?* he wanted to scream. A good moment to tell her had never arrived.

Apart from him, Mary Clare stood with her arms crossed, a slight frown on her face. Weariness?

Of course it is. He probably looked ragged, as did everyone who'd been awake twenty hours. With no sleep, she'd work in the kitchen—an hour from now. Likely, she was regretting her decision to stay out versus focus on the kitchen position.

"You could go," he whispered when Mr. Hortens started rounds.

She shook her head and paced alongside him. While Hortens checked the buds with the team leaders, Rivley and Mary Clare showed the growers pots that needed to be topped off to burn until the temperature rose above freezing.

Under the last tree, Mr. Hortens turned to them. "Thank you for your assistance overnight. I'll put in a word with Mistress Gere, especially regarding you, Miss Pemberton," he said to Mary Clare. "You aren't on staff, according to Mary Beth, so I'm even more appreciative you shared your smudging skills."

"I was glad to," murmured Mary Clare.

"My growers can handle the remaining hours. If they can't, they won't be with us much longer. Find your beds and rest." Mr. Hortens returned to his growers.

Rivley eyed Mary Clare. "Shall I walk you home?" He didn't dare suggest going to his room. A 'cambire would think nothing of the invitation, but who knew how a Knack-bearer would react?

She sighed. "Mary Beth said I could nap in her room."

"To the bunkhouse, then." He offered her his arm, and she rested her hand on it.

With a pale orange glow painting the sky in calmness, he didn't want to part from Mary Clare. He nudged them toward the workshop, hoping they could have a private word in warmth.

Once he closed the doors, Mary Clare wrapped her arms around his neck and kissed him.

Better than talking.

They took up where they'd left off in the orchard. Again, her hands found their way inside his coat, then *she* was inside his coat and unfastening her coat buttons. He helped. It *was* getting warm. He let her take the lead. She'd proven herself alpha several times, and he didn't want to mess this up by assuming 'cambire norms.

Sweaters dropped, leaving flannel shirts, his trousers and her bib and brace encumbering them. Her forwardness surprised him, then it became right. As she pressed ever closer, the sweet taste of her lips sent him soaring.

"Rivley?" she breathed.

Huh? Talking now was the last thing he wanted to do, but he pulled himself back to ground. "Mary Clare, you're so sweet, and...*this* is wonderful."

Her palm pressed to his chest, as if she was putting a stop to their activities. "I really like you. Like we're meant to be together."

"I like you, too. It's been a while since I've said that to anyone. I feel myself with you, so...natural with you."

Feel. The word shook Mary Clare from her happy cloud. While returning to the farmyard, she'd been careful and kept her Knack locked away. She checked it again. Walls still up. She grinned up at Rivley. This wasn't only her feeling this way. This was Rivley himself feeling he liked her.

His head dipped, and she answered with a kiss.

The kiss returned her to that lovely cloud. Her feelings enveloped her and carried her to *that* urge. It'd come and gone all night, and now it wouldn't go away.

Parting from his lips, she panted, "I want to... It's been a while, but I want to. So badly."

His lips came down on hers again, hard and pushing. She pushed back, and he returned with more, finally moving his hands where she wanted them to be.

Abruptly, he pulled away. "Are you sure?"

Her body was nearly erupting. "I...*yes*. Is there somewhere..."

With dawn shining through the shop windows, Rivley led her to the stack of canvas drop cloths and laid his coat across them. She dropped her coat beside his and unfastened the hooks on her bib and brace before sliding her hands around his waist and under his shirt again. *Ohhh—his muscular chest!* Smooth and sculpted, as fine as any she'd seen. She tugged his braces off his shoulders and laughed when he gasped as he noticed her bib and brace had puddled around her ankles.

On the makeshift bed, she giggled at his soft clicks. "What's this?" she asked, and when he stopped, she stroked his face. "Come on, it's sweet."

"It's avian." He shrugged. "It's a thing."

"A good thing?"

"Yep." He rolled them over and into a deep kiss. The clicking resounded through his chest, and she let the rhythm carry her, let his touch carry her.

"I love it," she gasped when she could, and then... "More. *Please.*"

• • •

MARY CLARE WOKE, warm and content…and happy. Very happy. The fog in her head cleared at the same time she realized someone was breathing against her shoulder. Her eyes flashed open. Rivley.

He was watching her, lit in the pink of sunrays bursting across the sky as if sharing their celebration.

"You're not late," he whispered. "I would have woken you."

"I, uh, thanks."

His lips twitched into a shy smile. Beneath that, he felt happier than he was letting on. *Very happy*. She'd been asleep, so… Her breath rushed out. Of course her Knack was open.

"How long?"

"That you slept, or until Mrs. Betsy arrives in the kitchen?"

She rubbed her head, trying to bring up her Knack walls. The darned things stalled—because she didn't want to push away this feeling, though it was the right thing to do. "Both?"

He caught her hand. "Don't worry, please. You slept about fifteen minutes, and we have a half hour." A wave of doubt wafted off him. "Are you… Is everything all right?"

If I haven't ruined it by not telling him. She was fairly sure the walls hadn't gone down until they'd…so that made it fine. She took his face in her hands and kissed him. "Everything was perfect. I feel"—oh, why did she say that?—"lovely. You?"

He brushed her hair from her forehead. "I would say I'm perfect as well. Er, I mean…*feel* perfectly." He returned the kiss.

A half hour. They had time.

As soon as she had the thought, *the desire*, he pressed against her. Argh, she couldn't. Not now, not swaying him. Not without telling him. The brush of cold metal reminded her of something she hadn't stopped to question earlier. She tapped the odd jewelry on his belly. "What's this?"

He stilled, but the real tell was his abrupt loss of wanting. This was…something.

"It's from back home. A talisman of an obligation I carry."

She sat up. "You're mated to someone?"

"No." Feathers broke out through his hair, raising it as he also sat up. And apart. "I'd like to tell you more, but when we have time."

In the growing light of dawn, she glanced at the silver spiral, and…er… *Look at the silver spiral.* He made no attempt to hide himself or it. A dark stone graced the center, and the metal twisted *through* his skin. A piercing.

She reached for her coat. "I hope its story is as fascinating as that talisman."

RIVLEY RAKED fingers through his hair. She needed to understand why he couldn't have a life mate. In fact, the gildan laid down opposite rules. He touched her shoulder, now covered in her woolen coat. "I want to explain."

"We need to talk, but I should wash up and go to work," she muttered and pressed her head again.

"You can use our spray washroom. Daeryn won't return until after sunrise." He dragged on his trousers, pulled up his braces and helped gather her clothes. Mary Clare followed him upstairs, quickly showered, and he showed her out again. He watched her cross the farmyard from the workshop.

Once she disappeared inside, Rivley returned to his room. He couldn't stay here, not with Daeryn returning, sniffing and knowing what he'd been up to. Instead, Rivley dropped his trousers and shifted.

Why didn't I tell her beforehand?

AS THEY FIXED BREAKFAST, Mrs. Betsy asked about the night's work, and Mary Clare answered her questions and reassured her the cherry crop would be fine.

"That's wonderful, duck! I canna imagine spring without

cherry pie." She exclaimed over jelly and other cherry recipes, blessing the workers and Mary Clare for pitching in.

Mrs. Betsy's talk became task directions, giving Mary Clare time to speculate on Rivley's mysterious obligation. Would it have been better to have known about it before they... Would knowing have changed anything?

Ha. Not after kissing him. By then, she'd known how much she liked him. She still liked him. She'd listen to his story and hope he'd listen to hers.

She swallowed. *And accept my Knack.*

CHAPTER 7

Soaring over the farm fields didn't ease Rivley's worry, but he caught two mice, so he didn't need to go inside for breakfast. By lunch, he'd worked up the nerve, but Mary Clare wasn't there.

He reviewed everything they'd said, every action he'd taken and her responses. Had she decided not to pursue the position here?

After an anxious afternoon of addressing the inventory—repeatedly losing focus and dropping things—he didn't want to attend dinner. In his present state, he'd make a fool of himself staring at her. But worse, what if she still wasn't there?

He lingered in the workshop until finally he had to know.

Mary Clare was clearing the platters when he arrived. Their gazes met. Shadows surrounded her tired eyes. She set down several dishes and nodded to a nearby chair. Then she disappeared. Not speaking—was she angry? The clink of dishes echoed around him. The room emptied. Each time she returned to collect the dirty dish tray, he scanned her face for clues, but she didn't meet his gaze again.

She was making sure he ate, leaving the food platters. That meant something, right?

The *thump* of boots approached, Wellspring's owner entering from her office across the hall. The tall woman still wore her split trouser-skirt and wellies, brown hair pinned in a roll.

"Still awake?" Mistress Gere asked gently. "I hope you had a nap after your work last night."

Holding his tea, Rivley nodded, though sleep hadn't come to his busy mind.

Smiling, she perched on an adjacent chair. "Mr. Hortens reviewed the night with his team leaders. They agreed the effort wouldn't have been successful without your hard work. I'll let Master Brightwell know he has a fine apprentice, and we'll increase your wages."

"You don't need to, ma'am."

"You have more responsibility than you did under Famil with the guards. We also discussed the…*workload* while Master Brightwell is away. You have the authority to decide which machines need to be in the shop."

Well, that was a relief. "Thank you, ma'am. And for the raise."

Saying good night, Mistress Gere continued to the kitchen. The clink of dishes stopped. A murmured conversation reached him. Then a squeal erupted, cut off quickly, but he recognized Mary Clare's excited voice.

He stood. He should leave. Talk to her later. Instead, he stepped closer to the fire so he wouldn't hear the conversation. Minutes later, Mistress Gere returned to her office.

Mary Clare rushed in. "Rivley. I'll be done in thirty minutes. See you then?"

He'd barely nodded when she picked up two platters and whirled away. She seemed more excited than upset. Had Mistress Gere paid her for last night's hours? They'd promised to talk, but a bad feeling about revealing his gildan swirled in his gut.

~

MARY CLARE WASHED DISHES, with Mrs. Betsy clucking beside her.

"Go home, duck. You need sleep."

But she wasn't going straight home, so it wasn't right to leave the dishes. Afterward, she hurried into her coat, said a quick good-bye and rushed out the door.

A few workers crossed the dusky farmyard, and a tall figure separated himself from the spreading tree in the center. She veered toward Rivley, with his pretty hair, freckled cheeks and broad shoulders. *Such a looker!* She pinched herself and gave a come-on wave. They needed somewhere private to talk.

He paced beside her, following along the southeast field. A stone wall separated the Collective from a neighboring pasture, mounted with wooden steps that she and her sisters used to go back and forth.

Arriving, she checked her wards again. All up. She'd had a momentary falter when Mistress Gere had given her the news, but she'd recovered. Facing Rivley, she leaned against the stile and clasped her hands. She'd never given the dangerous truth about her Knack to anyone outside the family.

"I have to—*want to*—tell you something about me that cannot be repeated to anyone."

He cocked his head, his eyes darting. "No one is nearby. Your secrets are safe with me, but you don't need to tell me anything you don't want to."

"That's the problem. If I want to continue seeing you, you need to know. And I'd like to see you more, Rivley."

He nodded.

Right, good. So now to tell him. She'd practiced the wording while mixing sauces and scraping bowls. *I have a Knack that sways people's emotions, and I likely swayed yours.* Yet, now those words wouldn't come out. "How are you feeling about us?" she blurted. "Honestly."

He rolled his eyes skyward, searching. "It's as if I've seen a mouse, and I'm hungry, but perhaps it's not my mouse. And if I catch the mouse, I still can't have it right now and maybe not for a long time. I'm not sure if I should dive down or not."

What? She stared at him.

He shrugged. "Well, you asked. The human response is probably 'unsure.' I'd like to court you, but I'm not certain you'll want to when I tell you my…situation."

She nodded knowingly. "I had the same thought about *my* situation. You may not wish to continue seeing me, because asking how someone is feeling is unnecessary for me." *It's now or never.* "I must lock away my Knack whenever I'm in public. Otherwise, it tells me folks' emotions. But when I sleep, or at private times"—she side-glanced to judge if he was catching on—"my wards can slip."

His gaze narrowed, his eyebrows becoming more pronounced. "So…you knew I had an interest in you before we even talked?"

"No, I was working. I had my wards up. But after we'd talked more and when we kissed the first time, they slipped." She shrugged. "Folks only kiss someone they like, so that wasn't secret, but…my Knack sends the feelings both ways. You might have noticed I was excited."

"I was excited," he said slowly. "Was that because of you?"

She swallowed. "That's why I asked if you'd hoped I'd join you *before* you came close to me. I wanted to make sure you liked me because it was your idea, not because I liked you."

He frowned.

"I don't do it intentionally," she said. "Most of the time, I can keep it in check, but your kiss was…rather nice. *Everything* was rather nice."

"I could tell. A fellow likes to have his *everything* appreciated." He grinned shyly.

Mary Clare wrung her hands. "I don't think you understand." She took a breath. "My Knack likely swayed your emotions."

"I understand."

So… He didn't *seem* angry. "You're still willing to see me?"

He crossed his arms. "How would I know you're influencing me?"

"It only happens if you're near me, three feet or less. I feel you and you feel me." She gestured between them. "The stronger emotion overwhelms the other. You'll come to know it's not you, and when you're away from me, the feeling disappears." She swallowed. "You learn to assess it. I had to."

His eyes turned a deep amber, and he stared into the distance, his features a mask.

Aw, damn it. He was upset. "I'm sorry," she whispered. "I-I'd appreciate it if you keep your word and not tell anyone." She mounted the steps to leave.

He caught her elbow. "Not all of the excitement came from you. I felt it away from you. Although I've never heard of such a thing."

She shrugged. "Who would tell anyone?"

"In Blighted Basin, no one is certain what Knacks are possible." He sighed. "I need to think about it, and you should hear my situation." His mouth crooked into a wry smile.

A bit of weight lifted from her shoulders. Nothing could be as bad as her Knack.

Rivley swiped his hand over his hair, flattening the feathers sticking through. Being with Mary Clare meant he'd have to be on his guard. His gaze roved over her clear green eyes, sweet lips and farther down. He suppressed a sigh. Yesterday had been the first he'd felt any connection to anyone since the accident.

Yet, had those been *his* feelings?

Itchy shifting feathers crowned his scalp. He pressed them again, weighing his choices. He didn't have any choice if he stopped now.

"Some of the gildan isn't my tale to tell, but my part is clear.

Daeryn and I share the obligation, lessons to resolve what went wrong on our team when a teammate died. As the alpha and beta of the team, we were responsible."

"I'm sorry for your loss."

He sighed. "Thank you. The point is, until the gildan is satisfied, we're banned from partaking in our traditional ceremonies."

"Some remote shires hold to old Basin traditions more than folks in the Farmland villages. I respect your beliefs," she said gently, "but you aren't in Rockbridge, so does it still matter?"

Rivley tapped his belly. "It's a blood-bound obligation. I can't take a life mate."

"Are you talking about us?" Her voice was low, incredulous. "Because I've known you a mere day. I'm interested in *courting*. Any future will be based on that."

The twitching urge to shift fell away. She wanted to…but what exactly did courting entail here and for a human? "Right, I'm interested in courting. But it's fair you know where I stand." He cleared his throat. "Daeryn may take years to address the lessons."

Mary Clare crossed her arms and frowned.

He fought the beta instinct to step back. But he was no longer a beta. He scoffed at himself—unfortunately aloud.

"What?" she huffed. "You can't start when *you* decide to resolve this bond?"

His shoulders stiffened. He couldn't back down from this alpha female. If they were to have balance in this relationship, he had to make his priorities clear. "That is between Daeryn and me. Do you seriously want to insert yourself? Because he doesn't favor *courting* humans."

Her gaze dropped to the ground. After a moment, she whispered, "You're right. It's not my business. You have to do what you feel is right for you."

He took a step closer. "Exactly. I left my home shire. I've taken a position folks back home have never heard of. I want to court a human when I'd never met one before coming to the Farmlands. Like me, you go after what you want. You're confident and skilled and not afraid to show it. I think we could get along if we have an understanding…about your situation and mine. What do you say? Should we give this a try?"

Mary Clare looked up at him, her hands now clasped behind her back. "I've gone after what I wanted. I learned to control my Knack so I could work outside the family, and now I've achieved that independence. Mistress Gere and Mrs. Betsy offered me the kitchen assistant position."

"Ho!" He grasped her shoulder, about to hug her…then realized they hadn't come to an agreement. But at her smile, he didn't draw back his hand.

"It was thanks to you asking me to help. They liked how I pitched in when I wasn't officially staff. Mrs. Betsy and I work well together, so Mistress Gere saw no reason to wait."

Her eyes were sparkling, but Rivley felt no excitement drifting from her.

"Tomorrow, I'll move into the bunkhouse, and I want you as a part of my new life."

Yes!

She put up a finger. "Yet, I can tell that if we're together, I'll immediately be shunned by jealous growers."

"You won't…" he started. "Ah, perhaps."

"You *are* quite the looker," she whispered.

"You're beautiful." He brushed a curl from her forehead.

"Maybe we could quietly court while we get to know each other?"

"Do you mean step back from"—he waved his hand between them—"activities like this morning's?"

She laughed. "Land's sake, you're so discreet! Not have sex? I don't want to stop—unless you want to?"

"Furthest thing from my mind." He gave a wry grin and tugged her closer.

Mary Clare looped her arms around his neck and met his kiss with a gentleness that lasted a wingbeat before it turned hungry.

Once again, Rivley felt the soaring sensation of being carried into the clouds. "I could get used to knowing how excited you are."

"Oops," she whispered against his lips. "Let me know if you spot your mouse."

Because the feeling was just right, he whispered back, "I think I have."

~

I hope you enjoyed this prequel novella with Mary Clare and Rivley. They and other characters living at Wellspring Collective are part of *The Luminated Threads* series. Perhaps you'd like to read more from this historical fantasy world?

The full story follows shapeshifter Daeryn and orphaned artist Annmar, accompanied by their friends Mary Clare and Rivley. The trilogy is written in the style of Victorian-era serialized fiction, made famous by Charles Dickens' installments in weekly or monthly periodicals. This means *The Luminated Threads* isn't neatly resolved in volume one. Have no fear, the story is complete within the three novels!

The Unraveling, Volume One of the Luminated Threads,
The Twisting, Volume Two of The Luminated Threads
and
The Binding, Volume Three of The Luminated Threads

~

ACKNOWLEDGMENTS

Thank you for reading *Falling into Place!* I had fun writing Mary Clare and Rivley's 'meet cute' because I could return to my favorite secondary characters from my first book world, *The Luminated Threads*! And I wrote it thanks to the pandemic!

I've been a member of local chapters of Romance Writers of America since 2007, and regularly attend workshops and writing events...or I did, up until March of 2020. Like everyone else in the new pandemic world, isolated writers began using zoom to replace our writing events. I joined an early morning sprinting group in April 2020, and after two years together we wanted to share our stories with the world. Naturally, our early meeting time played into the name of our anthology: *Love at Dawn!*

Thank you to my co-authors: J.T. Bock, G.G. Gabriel, Julie Halperson, Skye Knight, Meg Napier and J. Keely Thrall. All proceeds from our 2023 anthology went to **World Central Kitchen** to feed people in need in every corner of the globe. Thank you to my critique partners at CritiqueCircle.com who helped with revisions and polishing: Laura, Jason, Andy, Lizzie, Chuck, Chris, MeMy and Katie!

To keep in touch, hear about sales and be notified of future releases, please sign up for my newsletter on my website: www.laurelwanrow.com

ABOUT THE AUTHOR

Before kids, Laurel Wanrow studied and worked as a naturalist —someone who leads wildflower walks and answers calls about the snake that wandered into your garage. During a stint of homeschooling, she turned her writing skills to fiction to share her love of the land, magical characters and fantastical settings.

She's the author of *The Luminated Threads* series, a Victorian historical fantasy mixing witches, shapeshifters and a sweet romance in a secret corner of England, and *The Windborne*, a nature-focused YA fantasy series set in our world.

When not living in her fantasy worlds, Laurel camps, hunts fossils, and argues with her husband and two new adult kids over whose turn it is to clean house. Though they live on the East Coast, a cherished family cabin in the Colorado Rockies holds Laurel's heart.

Visit her website at www.laurelwanrow.com.

facebook.com/laurelwanrowauthor

instagram.com/laurelwanrowauthor

bookbub.com/authors/laurel-wanrow

pinterest.com/laurelwanrow